For all the children of the world.
May you know peace.

SEVEN SEAS
PRESS

Library of Congress Cataloging-in-Publication data available
ISBN 978-0-578-06443-7

The Three Sunflowers

by Janet Lucy

illustrated by
Colleen McCarthy-Evans

Dawn awoke early one morning
washing the summer sky in fresh new shades
of pink, orange and lavender.

As the sun rose over the low hill beyond the back fence,
the garden came alive with the happy hum of bees and butterflies
and the joyful trill of a red robin, brown sparrows and golden finches.

2

Gloria, a tall and regal sunflower,
had sprung up earlier in the season near the old pepper tree
where bird feeders hung from a crooked branch.

It wasn't long ago that she was a black and white seed
nestled in one of the feeders
destined to be food.

The messy diners at the feeders who frequented the garden all spring had scattered some of the seeds onto the ground where they became planted in the soil.

Now Gloria stood taller than ever,
welcoming Sunny and Solita,
the newest arrivals in the garden.

Gloria admired their fresh yellow petals, smooth as silk,
surrounding their faces like halos.
She delighted in their soft fuzzy centers,
each as distinct as a thumbprint.

Solita was just a head above Sunny,
who longed to catch up with her.

The garden was peaceful for the first few hours
of the day while the little trio of sunflowers
absorbed rich nutrients from the soil.

Over at the honeysuckle bush an iridescent green hummingbird flitted from flower to flower, sipping sweet nectar through its bill.

Nearby, the visiting goldfinches and house finches
chirped merrily as they pecked at the feeders.

Suddenly, a Cooper's Hawk, its eyes blazing like hot coals,
shattered the tranquility of the garden.
It shrieked as it swooped down on the feeders,
scattering the smaller birds in all directions.

"Oh no!" Solita cried out.

"Stop, stop, go away!" Sunny shouted.

The little birds flew off, wings aflutter,
while their tiny hearts pounded in their feathered chests.

"There are times in our lives when there is nothing we can do to prevent the chaos that surrounds us," Gloria gently explained to the young sunflowers.

"Then how can we help?" Solita demanded to know.

"We are sunflowers, golden and radiant," Gloria reminded them. "Our job is to be loving and peaceful wherever we stand."

The two young stalks shook beside her, frightened by the scene they had witnessed.

13

"Find a still point within you," Gloria guided them.
"Breathe all the way down into your roots."

"Is it gone?" Solita finally asked,
as her shaken stalk grew still.

"It's gone for now," Gloria assured her,
"and now is a perfect moment."

The garden was once again a peaceful place,
and harmony sang on a gentle breeze.

"Gloria," Sunny spoke up, "How do you know things?"

"I am taller than you, young one," she replied.
"I can see the world from a higher perspective."

"Will I grow taller and get bigger and stronger?"
Sunny wanted to know.

"Yes, you will find more strength," Gloria beamed at Sunny.
"You'll reach new heights and gain new perspectives too."

Gloria felt the youngster's tender leaves brush against hers.

Throughout the midday
the garden was happy and peaceful,
and the three sunflowers
beamed at the beauty
all around them.

"Brrrrr," Solita shivered,
as a gust of wind ruffled her soft silky petals.

The wind began to howl through the branches of the pepper tree, whipping and snapping at the feathery leaves and tiny red berries. Steely wool thunderclouds were rolling in, casting a dark shadow over the garden. Most of the inhabitants took refuge in their hideouts.
The three sunflowers remained where they stood.

The biggest cloud opened up with a roar
and rain poured down in giant buckets.
The sunflowers were tossed from side to side,
crashing into each others' faces and stalks.

"Gloria!" Sunny cried. "What's happening?"

"It's a late summer thunderstorm," Gloria explained.
"They can be a bit rough."

Water was quickly filling up the basin around them,
pooling into a puddle at the foot of their stalks.
Mud was softening around their roots,
and Gloria was beginning to tilt.

"You're slipping!" Solita cried. "You're going to fall over!"

"My roots are deep," Gloria assured her.
"Feel your own roots beneath you and reach down into the earth,"
she instructed Solita.
"Find the strength inside you, given to you by the sun."

Sunny shook and shuddered
but was determined to be brave.

Just then, spidery veins of lightning shattered the sky
and thunder boomed its response.

"The sky is cracking!" Sunny shouted,
bowing his head to protect his face.

"You're doing the right thing, Sunny,"
Gloria praised him.
"Fold your leaves and hold your body like a prayer."

"We are loved and protected by the Great Sun who created us, even when we cannot see the light through the darkness," she reminded them.

The young sunflowers held on by their roots, afraid they might collapse at any moment.

"If we fall to the ground our seeds will tumble into the earth, and we'll begin life again. Our cycle is endless," Gloria reassured them between claps of thunder. "And this storm will eventually pass."

Gloria reached for their slender stalks and pulled them close.

The three sunflowers huddled together,
like one big yellow umbrella swaying in the wind.

The dark afternoon turned to nighttime,
and the storm drummed on,
veiling the heavenly sky.

The moon watched faithfully
over the sunflowers
from behind her veil.

Dawn came early again the next morning
to survey the storm's damage.
The garden was still soggy,
and silence hung in the air like a misty blanket.

Beneath the pepper tree life began to stir.
The red-breasted robin pecked at the ground
and the little brown sparrow sang a greeting to the sky.

"That tickles," a little voice giggled.

"There's a butterfly on my face!" Sunny laughed.

"Shhhh," Solita whispered.
"We're giving thanks to the sun."

Gloria smiled.

And the three sunflowers stood still,
their faces turned upright,
grateful for another day in the garden.

To discover our Teaching Guide
filled with engaging activities and discussion questions for children,
please visit: thethreesunflowers.com

Sunflowers are an international symbol of PEACE.
Plant seeds for PEACE in your garden.

Janet Lucy, MA, is an award-winning writer and poet, and the author of *Moon Mother, Moon Daughter ~ Myths and Rituals that Celebrate a Girl's Coming of Age*, as well as *The Three Sunflowers* and *Mermaid Dreams (and their bilingual Spanish/English versions)*. Janet is the Director of Women's Creative Network in Santa Barbara, California, where she is a teacher, counselor/consultant, and offers women's writing groups and international retreats. She is the mother of two radiant daughters.

Colleen McCarthy-Evans is an award-winning creator of books and board games for children and families. She's a co-founder of The Santa Barbara Charter School, which teaches conflict resolution along with academics and the arts. She lives in Santa Barbara, California with her husband and dogs, loves to practice and teach yoga, and enjoys being in and out of the garden with her two grown sons, extended family and friends.

Heartfelt appreciation to our dear friends and loved ones
who offered their insights, inspiration and support
during the growing of the *The Three Sunflowers*.

Special thanks to Laurie Dean, Helena Hill and Patti Smart
for sharing their extraordinary gifts and expertise with us.

Our deepest gratitude to Patricia Selbert and Erika Römer
for affirming and manifesting our vision.

More book offerings by Janet Lucy, Colleen McCarthy-Evans and Seven Seas Press

Bilingual version

Bilingual version

Bilingual version

Games for families and teachers co-created by Colleen McCarthy-Evans

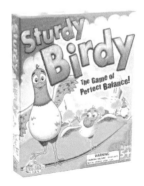  

CPSIA information can be obtained
at www.ICGtesting.com
Printed in the USA
LVRC101027230921
698554LV00002B/7